CW00864713

© Copyright 2015

Charming Billionaire
Bad Boy Billionaire

By: Grace Rawson

Charming Billionaire

Chapter One

Trent Buchanan swirled the rocks in his scotch and wondered why he thought he'd find a respectable date in a club like this. Not that this wasn't the hottest club in Manhattan. If he'd wanted the type that was hot, knew it, but pretended not to know it, he could have a dozen of options. Those wouldn't satisfy his mother.

She'd demanded that he bring a date to the fundraiser tomorrow night. She'd made it clear that she wanted marriage material. He had to bring Miss Right, not Miss Right Now. He sighed. He could flash a smile in any direction and have Miss Right Now purring on his lap.

Then he saw her. Across the room. What a cliché. As if a spotlight shone on her. Well it did. She'd walked through one as she traversed across the dance floor, avoiding the writhing bodies with her tray in her hand. That meant she was waitress. Not his usual type.

She was also a large, curvy girl. Trent didn't discriminate. He liked all women. He'd taken all shapes and sizes to bed. This girl had a determination in her step that piqued his interest. And red hair. He liked gingers. They had spunk. This girl strut across the place, in her silly and too-short-for-anyone cocktail waitress uniform, as if she owned the place. She rocked the outfit. No doubt about it. She worked those curves.

He finished his drink before she made it to his side of the bar. He signaled to her he wanted another one. He didn't but he needed to talk to her. He had to see fit here and had a brain and personality behind that body that didn't quit. Was she a potential Miss Right?

"What are you having?" she said.

Her nametag read, "Cassie."

"Scotch. The best you have."

She didn't roll her eyes, but Trent got the impression from her body language that she wanted to. "Coming right up."

She left him and he watched her ass as she walked away. He'd like to bite that, but he also thought his mother would believe she was his girlfriend. That she was marriage material. When she returned, he tried to engage her in conversation. She was not having it.

"I've got to make some tips tonight so I can't talk to just you," Cassie said.

He pulled out a fifty-dollar bill, putting it on the table. "Give me five minutes."

She eyed the bill as if calculating what she could do with that money. Trent had no idea what that felt like. He'd been born rich and had been successful enough to have his own money as an adult.

"Fine."

"So Cassie, what do you do besides waitress?"

She put a hand on her hip. "I race boats in the America's Cup. This job is so I don't lose touch with the common man."

She didn't smirk. Her ruby red lips didn't twitch. Her gaze never wavered from his. Trent let out a laugh. "Okay. I deserved that."

"As pickup lines, it isn't that original," she said.

He put a hand on his heart. "Ouch."

Cassie Hunt knew the type. This guy had never wanted for anything in his life. Now he thought he could buy her attention. Well, he could for five minutes. A quick fifty bucks. That money would go in her sock bank for the down payment on a condo.

She only had three thousand dollars to go. Then she'd have to work hard to get the next payment, but she'd figure that out then.

One day at a time. That's how she'd lived since her ex-boyfriend left town with her life savings.

Bastard.

He hadn't even been that good in bed. He'd been hung, but he'd had no idea what to do with it. Sad, really. All that dick and no way to pleasure a woman. Now this guy wanted her to flirt with him like he was a god. Men were all the same. Fragile egos.

She pasted on a smile, but she wasn't going to apologize for her snarky comment. He deserved it. Even if he was hotter than most rich guys who came to the club to pick up the beautiful women. He at least tried to look good with his jeans that might have been made for him, they fit so well. He had hair, not that being bald turned Cassie off. In fact, his hair looked good and devoid of product.

"Maybe because I'm not trying to pick you up in the usual sense," he said.

"What does that mean? You going to whisk me away and marry me?"

He laughed. Nervously. That put him in his place. She should just snatch that bill off the table and be done with him. He had three minutes left to wow her with whatever he was pitching.

"What if I am? Maybe I've fallen hopelessly in love with you and must have you. Make babies with you," he said.

What was his name? "Considering I don't even know your name, I'm not getting my hopes up for a marriage proposal."

"Trent Buchanan."

Of course. She'd guessed Chad or Biff. Trent would do.

"Look, Trent, you have about two minutes left before I've earned my fifty dollars. Why not get to the point?"

"Are you busy tomorrow night?"

She wasn't. She needed to find a new spot to park her car. That was it. That was her life.

"Yes."

He cocked his head. "Why do I think you're lying?"

"Because you can't fathom the idea that anyone would turn you down, let alone a fat girl turn you down."

He put his long-fingered hand back on his chest. "I'm hoping I get out of this conversation and I'm not bleeding."

She shrugged. "Your money. You didn't provide any parameters for what the conversation would entail. I believe you have thirty seconds left."

He handed her the bill. "We can end it here. I've enjoyed talking to you Cassie."

She tucked the bill into her bra then walked away, wondering what the heck that had been about.

Trent watched her go, that large ass swaying as she walked. He was intrigued, but he'd been shot down. There wasn't anyone else in the bar that was marriage material. Or no one who would look like marriage material to his mother. He sighed.

He had a full drink in front of him and a table of women eyeing him to his left. Nope. None of them would do. He sipped his drink knowing he could get drunk. His driver was only a text away.

But he didn't like to be drunk. Trent liked to be sharp at all times. One of the women from the table strode over to him. She was a leggy blonde with lips too big for her face. It actually made her more attractive. He braced himself for what her pickup line would be.

He also braced himself for the rejection she'd receive. He didn't get any joy in shooting them down, but he had to. He was on a mission tonight.

The exchange was pleasant and he hoped the woman went away thinking he wasn't a complete jerk. He wasn't. Most of his friends were, but his mother had raised him differently than that. He'd been taught that he wasn't better than anyone else.

His drink finished and the club about to close, Trent exited into a soft rain.

"Shit."

He looked around then followed the ranting voice into the alley next to the club. There she was. Cassie, in her cocktail outfit, looking a little bedraggled.

"What's wrong?"

She jumped. "Nothing."

"Clearly something is wrong," he said.

He approached her like a skittish horse. His hands were out in supplication. His steps remained slow and steady. She frowned and he stopped.

"I locked my keys in my car."

"Can someone come and bring you a spare," he said.

"No, there isn't anyone."

He sensed sadness in her words, but not in her posture. "Do you have a spare at home? I can drive you."

She shook her head, then looked down at her feet. She seemed to collect herself then looked him straight in the eye. "My car is my home."

How does that happen? He couldn't leave her here. "Then come home with me and you can get a locksmith to come out tomorrow in the daylight."

She blinked at him. "I'm not going to have sex with you. I'll figure something out."

"I'm not asking for sex," he said. "Though I'm not turning it down."

"I'm not that desperate."

"Oh, honey you are, but I have a business proposition."

A light drizzle began to come down. She put her arms around herself, clearly cold. He admired her spunk and her independence. His mother would certainly believe that she was who he'd pick to marry.

Not that he had any plans to marry.

"What kind of business proposition?"

"Let's get in my car and we'll talk about it."

Cassie eyed him as the rain began to come down harder. If she didn't find a shelter soon, she might be locked out for the night. This outfit was not fit for rain or cold. She could splurge for a hotel, but then that would take away from her down payment money.

She sighed. At least she could get out of the rain for the short term and regroup.

He'd pointed to the end of the alley.

"Okay," she said.

He led her to a stretch limousine. He opened the door and she hesitated for a minute. "I'll leave the doors unlocked. We won't move unless you're sure."

She nodded then climbed in. It was warm and had lights so she could see him better. Holy crap, he was hot. Dark hair, light eyes. Every hair in place. Yes, she wanted to dig her hands into it to mess it up. Her fingers itched with desire.

So did her vagina. She hadn't had that reaction to anyone in a long time. She squeezed her legs together to quell the feeling. Sleeping with this man should be the last thing on her mind.

"So, your business proposition," she said, wanting to distance him.

He sat across from her, giving her space. "You need something to drink?"

"No."

"Not even water?"

"No tell me your proposition."

He rubbed his hands on his well-creased trousers. "I have to go to a fundraiser tomorrow and I need a date."

"You can't get a date?"

She laughed. She couldn't help it. He smiled at her. "I can get a date. I need one that will make my mother think that I'm going to settle down."

"You need an almost fiancé."

"Yes."

Okay. She could pretend to be in love with this hot man. Wouldn't be hard. "What do I get out of this?"

He cleared his throat. "A million dollars and a warm place to sleep. No sex. No strings."

"How long do I have a warm place to sleep?"

She might come cheap, but she wasn't going to be easy. She had more self-respect than that. On the other hand, truth be told, if he looked at her the right way, she might sleep with him. Tonight.

"For as long as it takes you to find your own place."

She tapped a finger on her lips. This was a good deal. With a million dollars she would have her down payment and then some. If she stretched it properly she could find a better job than waitressing.

"Okay."

He smiled, clearly relieved. "Then let's go to my place. Is there someone you want to call to let them know where you are?"

She quirked an eyebrow at him. She wasn't sure if he was fishing or just being a gentleman. "Yes. What's the address?"

She texted a friend, then tucked her phone back into her bra.

"Good." He held out his hand. "For now we'll shake. I'll draw up the contract when we get to my place."

Chapter Two

For someone who was living in her car with all of her belongings, Cassie had negotiated like a professional. Was it desperation or was she that sure of herself? Trent wanted to get to know her better. He already like Cassie.

"What's your last name?"

"Hunt."

They were almost to his penthouse. He'd call a locksmith tonight and pay whatever was necessary. He'd have someone bring her car here. That way she wasn't stranded. His driver parked the car in the garage under his building.

Trent leaned against the wall of the elevator, studying Cassie as they rode to the top of the building he owned.

"Like what you see?" she said.

She didn't look at him.

"I do. Very much. You're a beautiful woman, Cassie. Is that short for Cassandra? She was in Troy given the gift of foresight, but with the curse that no one would believe her."

"You don't need to be charming. I agreed to be your pretend fiancé already."

"Should I be mean then?"

"No, just don't say everything like you're trying to get me into bed."

Trent chuckled. "But that's who I am. A guy always trying to get a woman in to bed."

"Nice of you to be honest, but you can save the charm for someone else. I'm not sleeping with you. Besides I'm sure I'm not your type."

The elevator doors opened into his apartment. It was two floors with a view to die for. Cassie gasped.

"What is my type?"

She glanced at him then walked to the windows. She clearly liked the view. "Blonde, big boobs. Skinny because she doesn't eat or she's thrown up everything she has ever consumed."

"I'm a little more well-rounded than that. I like all shapes and sizes."

She spun around to look at him. "When was the last time you did a girl who was a size eighteen?"

He had to think about it. Maybe he hadn't been in bed with someone quite that big. "I don't know. I don't check the dress size as I'm taking it off of her. I have other things on my mind. Like seeing that dress pooled at her feet."

She licked her lips. He might just be getting to her. He liked a challenge. Too many women fell madly in bed with him. Too easy. If he had to work for the fuck, he would enjoy it more. And Cassie's surrender to him would be sweet.

Or would it? He suspected that she lived life on her terms and that the same would happen when she was in his bed. He might have to watch out of this one. She was a game changer.

She stepped closer to him, within his personal space. She smelled like peaches. Her lips hovered over his and he parted his anticipation of her kissing him. Come to papa.

"I need something to change into."

Her breath wafted across his face. She was close enough that he could see her green eyes sparkle right before she stepped away from him. He cleared his throat and needed to adjust himself, but he wasn't going to give her the satisfaction of letting her know she'd made him hard.

"Uh, I'm sure I can find some sweats."

She glanced down his body. "Once you're out of the room, you can adjust yourself."

Her laughter went through him, making him even harder.

Cassie watched him walk away, his stride odd because she knew he was as hard as a rock. He had a nice ass. A really nice ass. She'd like to have both of her hands on that ass as he pounded into her. Bet he was good in bed.

He'd probably had enough practice to be an expert. If sex were a video game, he'd be on the expert level by now. Her panties were wet just thinking about him.

He returned with a pair of sweat pants and a shirt. He handed them to her. He was walking better now.

"Thanks. I want to take a shower."

He pointed over his shoulder. "There are three bathrooms down the hallway. Pick which one you want." He leaned in closet to her his lips a hair's breadth away from her ear. "The last one is mine."

She swallowed. "And if I choose that one?"

"You won't be showering alone."

His voice came out gravelly and she knew she was affecting him, still. She smiled sweetly at him as she bounced out of the room. And went directly to his bathroom.

If she was going to be here with a hot guy, she might as well have fun with it. She turned on the water to warm then stripped of her waitress uniform. Next she folded her underwear neatly on a shelf beside the shower.

"You look pretty good naked," he said from the doorway. He'd loosened the tie he'd been wearing.

"You might as well wait," she said as she entered the stall. "Shower sex is complicated enough. More so with a big girl."

She slid the translucent door closed, putting her face under the spray. The door moved open then he was there. His body heat warmed her up. Not that the space was cramped. Several of her would fit in here.

With several more of him. As she stood under the spray, he tugged at the band that held her hair back. He then stuck his face in her long, red tresses. "I love long hair."

She didn't want to move. His fingers were working magic on her scalp.

"May I wash your hair?"

"Yes," she whispered. Anything to prolong his strong fingers on her body.

He began to rub her scalp, getting every part of it. She moaned. All he was touching was her head. What was going to happen when he touched other things? Things she was going to encourage him to touch.

Chapter Three

Trent liked Cassie's hair and she'd moaned. She was going to do that a lot more of that tonight if he had any say in it. One hand was braced on the shower wall. The other rested on the door. Both in fists. Oh yeah. She was turned on.

So was he. His erection nudged her back. That ass was even better up close. Miles of pales skin. And a few freckles right above her crack. Leaving one hand on her head, he leaned downed, kissed them. She jumped.

"Like that?"

"You just surprised me," she said.

He chuckled. "I may not have shower sex with you, Cassie, but we're going to right afterward."

He saw her shiver. He let her hair rinse out in the flow of water. She turned, her green eyes just a little darker. "This has nothing to do with our contract."

His lips hovered over hers. "Two different things, but one will help the other."

"Oh?"

"If you are attracted to me then you won't have to fake it," he said.

"I've never faked it."

"No one has ever had to fake it in my bed," he said.

A smile flickered across her lips before he took possession of them. Those full lips were magnificent. Soft and warm and responsive to him. What would they look like wrapped around his cock?

She jammed her fingers in his hair, pulling him closer. Her body was warm and supple. Damn. She was good with that mouth.

"Oh, Cassie," he said when he let go of her lips. "This is going to be a lot of fun."

He loved that she didn't break from his gaze. She was going to have fun and she wasn't going to apologize for it.

"Let's finish this shower then get down to business," she said.

He'd never seen anyone wash so quickly. He just leaned against the shower wall, enjoying the view. Especially the one where she bent to soap up her legs. His dick was alive now. He dried her off. She dried him off and then he was racing to the bed with her in tow.

"Now I take my time," he said.

Her eyes sparkled. "Oh? Do I get a say in this?"

"You tell me to stop, I will."

"I don't think stop is the word that I'll use. More like hurry."

"That I won't do. We have all night, Cassie. I hope you don't have big plans for tomorrow because you might not be sleeping tonight."

She cocked an eyebrow at him. "I'll believe it when I see it." She ran her finger down the middle of his chest igniting fires wherever she touched. "Or feel it."

He wanted to throw her down and pound into her, but he was going to be slower than that. No need to hurry. He didn't have to get up in the morning and frankly, she shouldn't have to either. He was paying her enough to be his date so that she didn't have to work for awhile.

He knelt in front of her and took one large nipple into his mouth. Both hands held her breast firmly so he could worship it properly. Her fingers held his shoulders and a low keening sound came out of her mouth. He chuckled against her breast.

This was better than surrender. This was someone who wanted to be here.

Oh, Trent's mouth. Oh, his tongue. What it was doing to Cassie. She wasn't sure she could stand for much longer. She wanted him. Inside of her. Now.

"Trent."

"Be patient, baby."

Baby? No one called her that. Sounded good coming out of his mouth. Then he began to work on her other breast. Oh, mother of pearl. When would this sweet torture end?

She arched her body into him and heard his chuckled as well as felt it against her chest. He was enjoying this. He wanted to drive her crazy. This was probably more foreplay than she had with all of the lovers, combined. Trent was going to take his time and no amount of squirming on her part was going to change that.

"Holy crap," she said as he bit her nipple.

Her body shuddered.

"Your breasts are so beautiful," he said.

He was standing now, nudging her onto the bed. She lay on it, already close to boneless and he hadn't even entered her. This man was already an amazing lover. And he had a cock that could probably satisfy her. More than once.

He knelt again, this time between her legs.

"A natural redhead."

He licked her folds, creating a buzzing in her ear. Oh God. The tension built. It had been ages since anyone had given her pussy a proper licking. Trent was doing more than that and she felt as if the rest of her body had gone numb. She didn't think she had any other body parts beside her clit.

That was where all of her awareness was focused.

And then she was over the edge. Flying and not caring when she landed. Or if she ever landed.

"Slide up, Cassie," Trent said.

With flailing limbs, she slid further onto the giant bed. She heard the rip of a condom pack then when she looked, Trent was rolling it onto himself. She hadn't even had to beg. She hadn't even had to ask. So different from the other men who'd taken her to bed.

Most of them she'd had to convince to use protection. They'd assumed she was a virgin and therefore clean. Trent hadn't.

He climbed on top of her. "Ready?"

She smiled. "Of course. Unless you aren't."

He nudged her with his erection. "I think that is a rhetorical question."

She laughed. He slid inside of her then stopped. His eyes fell closed. She wanted him to move more than she wanted to take her next breath.

"I need a moment," he said when she arched her body into his. "You feel so good, Cassie."

He felt pretty good, too and would feel ever better when he was moving.

Chapter Four

Oh, my goodness was all Trent could think. Then he began to move inside of her. She arched to meet his every stroke. In and out, but he didn't want it to end. He could spend the rest of his life right here. Never leaving her pussy.

Damn.

He braced his hand on either side of her head, kissing her as he slid in and out. She moaned. She keened. He moaned. He almost keened, but thought it might not be manly.

Her legs wrapped around him. He sped up without consciously deciding to. She surrounded him and he could die a happy man.

But he wasn't going to die. No he wasn't. He wasn't going to hold out any longer with the sexy noises she was making. Then she arched more than before and her vagina clenched around him. He was done for and followed her over the edge, thrusting like a man who had nothing to lose.

Then silence except for their ragged breaths. He buried his face in her neck, taking in her wondrous smell. Too bad he had to move. Get rid of the condom.

He did so with as little movement as possible. Then he was back next to her, touching her as if she weren't real.

She was a living, breathing beautiful woman that had managed to give him an orgasm that almost made him believe in a higher being. Her hand rested on his chest and he laced his fingers with hers.

An affectionate gesture that he never did out of bed. He'd certainly never done it in bed. But Cassie was different. He'd known this all along. From the moment he'd seen her in that spotlight. What was his heart going to do?

This was new territory for him. At this point, he'd count to one hundred then leave if he was at the woman's place. If there were here, he'd call them a cab or have his driver take them home.

This time, he knew that Cassie wasn't leaving. She could have another room to sleep in, he had plenty, but he wanted her right here. For as long as he could have her.

Cassie leaned on her elbow. "This is usually where the guy runs away. Slinks out. Makes his excuses."

How sad that she'd been on the other end of what he'd done to some many. He brushed a hair out of her face. "What are you saying? I should go?"

She laughed. "Hardly. It's your place. I'm asking if you want me to sleep in another bedroom."

There was no sadness in her eyes. Just a resignation of her reality.

"No. I want you right here, Cassie. I want to wake up and make love to you again."

Make love? Had he ever called it that? Had she put a spell on him?

"I don't mind," she said. "You have a few to choose from."

She began to sit up. He snagged her arm. "Stay."

She looked him over then nodded. "Okay."

His heart leapt. His body rejoiced. He snugged her up against him then feel asleep.

Cassie woke and had no idea what time it was. The sun was streaming in through the blinds on the big window. She knew where she was. She knew what had gone on last night. Three times. Three times. And each time she'd cum twice. Six orgasms in one night.

Her body ached in a very good way. She reached for Trent, but he wasn't there. Her body sighed, a little sad. He must have had regrets in the light of the morning. Then she smelled coffee. She sat up. Her stomach rumbled. Bacon? Was that bacon?

A red robe had been tossed across the bottom of the bed. Looked to be her size, so Cassie put it on. And her body had a robegasm. It was the softest robe she'd ever worn and yes it fit her.

"Oh."

She left the bedroom to find Trent. If he was still here. He stood in the kitchen in nothing but jeans that might have been grown on him like a second skin. Not too tight, but they hugged his wonderful ass. That's all he wore. Jeans.

His chest had a light smattering of hair that grew thicker as it went south.

"Like what you see?"

Cassie jumped. Trent was smiling at her as if he knew she'd been checking him out. "I do."

"How do you take your coffee?"

"Cream and one sugar," she said.

He poured her some, then fixed it how she'd said. Before handing it to her, he gave her a kiss. "Good morning."

"Good morning." She sipped the coffee and her taste buds did a happy dance. "This is good."

"French Press. The only way to make coffee. You want some eggs? Pancakes?"

"Eggs are fine. However you are having them," she said.

She slid onto a stool at the breakfast nook. Trent had turned to her, hands on his hips. "How do you want your eggs, Cassie?"

She eyed him. "Doesn't matter. Do I look like I'm a picky eater?"

"Cassie, tell me how you want your eggs. I want to know. I want to cook them how you want them."

She blinked. Why was this so important to him? "Uh fried, sunny side up."

"You want toast."

"Don't go to any trouble."

"Holy shit, Cassie. Don't pull that with me. If I ask you what you want, I actually want to know. Whether it is in bed or in the kitchen or any room."

"Yes, toast. Okay?"

"Good."

He walked over then kissed her on the lips. "Don't ever brush off what I ask, Cassie. Always tell me."

"Okay."

He smiled then went back to cooking for her. Cassie wasn't sure what had happened, but she knew that she had judged Trent wrong. He was rich, but he was probably the nicest rich man she'd ever met.

Chapter Five

With breakfast and showers finished, Trent knew that they needed to get some work done.

"We need to go shopping," Trent said. He pulled a key from his pocket. "And your car is in the garage downstairs. You can get anything you need from it now."

She looked at him as if he'd just given her a present. "You took care of this? Thank you."

"Of course. Why wouldn't I?"

She blinked, but seemed unable to put things into words. "Just thank you. Why do we have to go shopping?"

"Because you need a dress for the fundraiser tonight. I would imagine that you don't keep your fancy dress gowns in your car."

They stood in the hallway outside the front door. "I hadn't thought about a dress."

"Well I did. We'll get you a dress. Pedicure, manicure. You can have your hair done, too if you want." She just stared at him. "Go get your purse. The car is down stairs."

"Uh, okay."

What was her problem? It was a day of pampering for her. She came back with shoes on and her purse in her hand. He'd found her another outfit to wear which fit her better than he would have hoped.

"Let's go."

"Can I ask you a question?" she said when they were going down in the elevator.

"Sure."

"Why me?"

"What do you mean?"

"Why did you pick me to be your pretend fiancé?"

He rubbed his chin. "There was something real about you. Something different than the women I usually bring home to mother. Oh, they've all tried to act like they loved me and not my money, but you didn't seem to care that I was rich. You knew it, I assume."

"I knew you were rich." She waved her hands around. "I didn't know you were this rich."

"Would you have treated me differently?"

"I might have avoided your table."

He laughed. "I admire your honesty."

The elevator doors opened. Trent ushered Cassie out to the car. He took her to his sister's favorite dress shop. She stopped right before they entered. "Is the cost of all of this deducted from my million?"

Trent smiled. "No, it isn't. Trust me. Don't look at the price tag."

"You do understand that this store will probably not have my size. Most likely it doesn't go above a twelve. I'm bigger than that."

"There are such things as alterations," he said.

"They'd have to combine two dresses."

He put a hand on her arm. "You aren't that big. You're curvy. That's it."

She eyed him as if not believing him. She wasn't as big as she acted. Yes, she had curves. He liked curves. Made sex way more interesting.

"If you want to think so, that's sweet."

He held the door open for her, cursing the men in her life that had made her feel that way. She was a beautiful, smart woman. Why has someone degraded her? Why had men seen fit not to see that? Men were truly pigs.

To Cassie's surprise they did have her size in the shop Trent brought her to. She currently had on a flirty red dress that she felt like a queen in. She couldn't stop looking at herself in the mirror. She actually thought she was beautiful.

"You face says it all," Trent said. He was standing behind her, looking in the mirror.

"You tore yourself away from your phone."

He'd been on it all morning.

"I'm not this rich because I sit on my ass all day. I have business to conduct. A company to run."

There was no rancor in his voice. Just a firmness that let her know she shouldn't bring it up again. Fair enough. She was benefiting from all that working he did.

"What did you mean by my face says it all?"

She turned to him. He turned her back to the mirror. "This is the biggest smile I've seen on you since I've met you."

He wasn't wrong. This was probably the biggest smile she'd had on her face in a long time. She wasn't a girly girl, but she liked how she looked. He leaned closer and whispered, "You see yourself as sexy and beautiful. This might be the closest you'll ever get to see yourself as I see you."

She couldn't stop smiling. She'd underestimated him.

He turned to the salesperson who had been lurking nearby. "We'll take this. Do you have it in blue also?"

"Yes sir."

"Throw the blue one in also and she'll need shoes also and some accessories."

"Oh, Trent. Don't go overboard," Cassie said.

"When was the last time anyone spoiled you?"

She couldn't remember anyone spoiling her. Well her father had, but then he'd died and that had stopped. He was probably the last person who had told her that she was beautiful. Cassie sniffed as Trent walked away with the salesperson. She wasn't going to cry, but she'd never felt this special. She'd never thought feeling this way was important.

She'd miss this when this was all over, but then again, she'd never let anyone treat her badly ever again. Maybe if her father had lived, she might have never let anyone treat her as less than special.

The woman came back with shoes. Not too tall, but strappy and shiny. Cassie tried them on as well as the necklace and bracelet the woman offered. They all completed the outfit.

"Mr. Buchanan had to take a call. He said he'd be out in a few minutes. I can ring this up in the meantime."

Cassie must have given her a strange look because the woman patted her shoulder. "He gave me his credit card."

Cassie blew out a breath. She hadn't looked at the price tag, but she was sure that it was more than she made in a year. She changed back into her street clothes. By the time she was done Trent was off the phone and signing the credit card slip. He tucked it in his pocket before she could see the total.

He smiled, took the bags in one hand, then offered her his arm with the other. "Ready?"

Chapter Six

Because so many of his dates had liked him, at first, for his money, then his abilities in bed, Trent had never taken anyone on a shopping trip. This was actually fun. He had to conduct business on his phone and through e-mails, but he didn't care. Just to see Cassie's face today had been wonderful.

He looked in the mirror one more time to make sure that his bow tie was straight. What a great day they'd had. He could imagine himself doing that for Cassie on a regular basis, but he assumed she'd want to take her money and go back to her life.

He had no idea what her life had been other than living out of her car. She wouldn't need to do that again. Maybe he would have to talk to her. He'd never met anyone like Cassie. Strong and sexy and smart. He realized that he had no idea what her ambitions were.

He left his bedroom, then knocked on her door. She'd chosen to dress in one of the other bedrooms. She opened the door and the sight took away his breath.

"Wow."

"You like?" she said.

"If we didn't have to be there I would strip off that dress and do naughty things to you."

She didn't blush. At all, but from the look on her face, she was debating letting him do it. He grabbed her hand. "Let's go before I call my mother and beg off. She'd never forgive me. Besides, we need to talk."

"Oh?"

He stopped. "No, no. Not that kind of talk. We need to get to know each other. We don't have to be engaged tonight, but we need to know some things about each other."

"My favorite color is purple. I was born in Pennsylvania. My mother is alive and living in Florida," she said. "I went to NYU and graduated with a degree in finance."

"Finance?"

"Yes, finance. Sadly they don't teach you how to choose a good boyfriend at college. I chose badly and he wiped me out," Cassie said.

She owned her mistakes and he had to admire that. He squeezed her hand. "That boyfriend is long gone."

He filled her in on some details of his life as they rode down in the elevator. She told him some of her background as they drove to the fundraiser.

"What are you raising money for?" Cassie asked, as Trent helped her out of the limousine.

"I think tonight is cancer."

"You go to more than one of these a year?"

"I go to more than one of these a week sometimes. At least tomorrow is Saturday. We can sleep in for sure."

"I have to go to work," she said.

"I'll give you a bonus if you spend the day with me."

She bit her lip. "No bonus needed to persuade me to do that."

Did Trent think he had to pay her for everything? How did she tell him that she was enjoying herself immensely with him? The night out had gone quickly. She'd met Trent's family and they all had been warm and sweet to her. Made her feel guilty for lying to them about her relationship with Trent.

At the end of the night, Cassie felt like Cinderella except her carriage wasn't going to turn into a pumpkin. Too bad this wasn't going to be her carriage for much longer. She'd fulfilled her obligation and now she had to find a place to live.

The idea of leaving Trent made her sad. She wanted to stay with him because she was falling in love with him. She didn't want to tell him because he might kick her out early.

He leaned toward her in the back of the car. "You're deep in thought."

"I guess I better start looking for a place to live tomorrow," she said.

He frowned. "There is no hurry. I'm not going to kick you out."

"Still. The agreement was for this date and now this date is done."

"I haven't transferred the money yet."

"I have no doubt that you will. I trust you," she said.

She didn't want to think about leaving, but she had to be practical. She'd been homeless and now she didn't have to be.

"How about we go home, have a bath and think about tomorrow when it comes," he said.

"I'm a planner."

"You can plan in the morning. I'm not kicking you out. You can stay as long as you need to. Besides, you already promised to spend the day with me. If you want, we can go look at apartments."

She mulled that over. Might not be bad to have a second opinion on a place. "Okay."

"Good. We'll think about it tomorrow."

She laughed. She doubted that he approached his business that way. They arrived at his apartment building. "What do you do for a living?"

"I wrote an app that sold well. Now I'm running a computer security business," he said.

"Okay. I don't know enough about either of those things to ask any more questions."

He chuckled, then kissed her. "I don't think that it would be that interesting."

"If people enjoy what they do then it is interesting to listen to them talk about it."

"Let's talk tomorrow. Tonight is about you and me," he said.

She liked the look of passion on his face. She'd inspired that. Gave her a sense of empowerment that she could make a man that turned on and she hadn't taken off her clothes. He held her hand then led her into his bathroom.

"Please stay right there."

She did as he said while he filled the bathtub with water.

Chapter Seven

Trent didn't think he'd ever seen a more beautiful woman in his life. Not just outside, but inside also. She'd charmed his family and that made him feel a little guilty for lying to them. His sister had sent him a text that said Cassie was a keeper.

Why did he think that also? She was a great woman. Smart and maybe he could help her find a job in finance. He'd bet she'd prefer that to waitressing.

Or he could just ask her to stay. Would she do that? He could invent things and run companies, but asking this woman to stay in his life scared the crap out of him. Not because she might say yes, but because she might say no.

The bathtub was full and he'd put bubbles in it.

"You want champagne?"

"You have some?"

"Always. Don't move."

He came back with the bottle and two glasses. He wanted this to be perfect. He hadn't ever wanted to be this romantic, but he felt his life depended on it. If Cassie saw him as someone other than a playboy, she might consider giving them a try.

She smiled at him when he returned. "Can I at least sit?"

"Of course, yes."

He opened the champagne then poured two glasses as she sat on the tile surrounding the tub. He handed her one then clinked his with hers. She smiled before she sipped. He put his glass down then took of his jacket, shirt and shoes. He held out his hand for her.

He wanted to undress her slowly. Enjoying the reveal. She shifted off her shoes. The dress was perfect for her. He kissed her, then unzipped the dress, but he couldn't bring himself to just let it pool at her feet. Instead he folded it nicely.

He admired her for a moment. "Perfection. I really like the red bra and panties. One of these days I want you to just wear them and the shoes, but I know your feet must hurt from having them on all night."

"Yes, they do. I'm a sneakers kind of gal."

"We'll have to explore that side of you also."

"We only have one night."

Not if Trent had anything to do with it. He took off her bra then slid her panties down her legs. He held out his hand. "Your bath, milady."

She giggled then stepped into the tub. "You aren't going to cannonball into the tub are you?"

"Now there's a thought."

She laughed and he felt that laugh to his soul. She was a witch. She'd cast a spell on him. He'd never felt like this before, with anyone. He undress then slid in at the opposite end of the tub. "Come here. Lean against me."

She did. He hooked her legs around his and then spread her wide. "This one's for you and only you."

"You don't have to."

"I want to Cassie. I want you to know how beautiful you are and just how much in life you deserve."

Cassie rested her head on Trent's shoulder and thought that she'd fallen in love with this man. He'd done this to her. He hadn't looked at another woman all night. And a number of them had thrown themselves at him. He'd acted as if he hadn't even noticed. She'd noticed the daggers in her back all night.

And here Trent was, his fingers sliding down her torso to pleasure her. He reached his destination and began to rub slow circles over her clit. Her body began to hum. She gripped the sides of the tub. Her body wanted to arch into his hand. His other hand held her steady.

She felt vulnerable and safe at the same time. The buzzing began in her ears and she was going to scream with her release.

"Oh, God."

He chuckled in her ear.

Then she was over the cliff. How did he do that so easily? Her body spasmed for a few minutes before she recovered.

"I could do that every day," Trent said.

"That was amazing."

"Good. And I did that for a reason."

"Why?"

Her voice was small because she hadn't truly caught her breath yet.

"I want you to have no resistance."

"What?"

That woke her up.

"Cassie, please stay with me."

She sat up, turning to look at him. "What?"

He put his hands on her face. "I'm in love with you. Please stay. Stay tomorrow and the next day and let's see where this leads. I think we can be so happy together."

"You're in love with me?"

She knew a smile broke out on her face. Was she hearing him properly? Was this avowed bachelor in love with her? Cassie Hunt. Plus sized girl. Is she really going to get the guy? Seemed implausible, but he would have no reason to lie to her.

"Yes."

His eyes searched hers.

"I love you too, Trent. I'll stay."

"Then let's get out of here and make this official."

"Huh?"

"I mean in bed. We can talk about marriage and all that later."

Her head spun as he helped her out of the water. He was already hard, but she needed a minute. "Marriage."

"If you are open to it, but this isn't a proposal. When I do propose I'm going to do it right."

Proposal? She sat down on the edge of the tub. "You're serious?"

"Very serious, Cassie. I can't imagine my life without you."

His eyes had grown dark again. He hadn't let go of her hand. She'd never thought that she would get married. "You want to marry me?"

"Yes, but this isn't the proposal. I don't know how I'll do it, but it'll be big and memorable."

Oh. My. God. She jumped up then kissed him hard. He stumbled back a little. Guess she'd been enthusiastic. This man, who she'd thought was just a rich jerk, was far more than that. And he was all hers.

"Take me to bed, Trent."

He laughed. "We'd be there if you hadn't sat down."

"I won't make that mistake again. I promise.

THE END

Don't miss out!

Click the button below and you can sign up to receive emails whenever Grace Rawson publishes a new book. There's no charge and no obligation.

Sign Me Up!

http://books2read.com/r/B-A-RWSC-SLWI

BOOKS 2 READ

Connecting independent readers to independent writers.

15159829R00025

Printed in Poland
by Amazon Fulfillment
Poland Sp. z o.o., Wrocław